Ulysses
James Joyce

This extract first published in the UK in 2003
exclusively for WHSmith Limited,
Greenbridge Road, Swindon SN3 3LD
www.WHSmith.co.uk

by HarperCollins*Publishers*

To celebrate the BBC's The Big Read

Cover design template
copyright © 2003 WHSmith Limited
Cover illustration copyright © Bee Willey

ISBN 0 00 717446 2

Typeset by Palimpsest Book Production Limited,
Polmont, Stirlingshire

Printed and bound in Great Britain

This is the first section of the first chapter
of *Ulysses*.

'*Ulysses* is the book to which we
are all indebted and from which none
of us can escape.'

T.S. ELIOT

James Joyce was born in Dublin in 1882, but for most of his life lived in self-imposed exile in Paris, Trieste and Zürich. Controversy and critical acclaim in equal weight accompanied the publication of each of his books, but none more so than *Ulysses*, published in Paris in 1922 despite difficulties with printers, publishers and censors. Joyce died in Zürich in 1941.

I

STATELY, plump Buck Mulligan came from
the stairhead, bearing a bowl of lather on
which a mirror and a razor lay crossed. A
yellow dressing-gown, ungirdled, was
sustained gently behind him by the mild
morning air. He held the bowl aloft and
intoned:

    —*Introibo ad altare Dei.*

Halted, he peered down the dark winding
stairs and called up coarsely:

    —Come up, Kinch. Come up, you fearful
jesuit.

Solemnly he came forward and mounted
the round gunrest. He faced about and
blessed gravely thrice the tower, the

surrounding country and the awaking mountains. Then, catching sight of Stephen Dedalus, he bent towards him and made rapid crosses in the air, gurgling in his throat and shaking his head. Stephen Dedalus, displeased and sleepy, leaned his arms on the top of the staircase and looked coldly at the shaking gurgling face that blessed him, equine in its length, and at the light untonsured hair, grained and hued like pale oak.

Buck Mulligan peeped an instant under the mirror and then covered the bowl smartly.

—Back to barracks, he said sternly.

He added in a preacher's tone:

—For this, O dearly beloved, is the genuine Christine: body and soul and blood and ouns. Slow music, please. Shut your eyes, gents. One moment. A little trouble about those white corpuscles. Silence, all.

He peered sideways up and gave a long low whistle of call, then paused awhile in rapt attention, his even white teeth glistening here and there with gold points. Chrysostomos. Two strong shrill whistles answered through the calm.

—Thanks, old chap, he cried briskly. That will do nicely. Switch off the current, will you?

He skipped off the gunrest and looked gravely at his watcher, gathering about his legs the loose folds of his gown. The plump shadowed face and sullen oval jowl recalled a prelate, patron of arts in the middle ages. A pleasant smile broke quietly over his lips

—The mockery of it, he said gaily. Your absurd name, an ancient Greek.

He pointed his finger in friendly jest and went over to the parapet, laughing to himself. Stephen Dedalus stepped up, followed him wearily halfway and sat down on the edge of the gunrest, watching him still as he propped his mirror on the parapet, dipped the brush in the bowl and lathered cheeks and neck.

Buck Mulligan's gay voice went on.

—My name is absurd too: Malachi Mulligan, two dactyls. But it has a Hellenic ring, hasn't it? Tripping and sunny like the buck himself. We must go to Athens. Will you come if I can get the aunt to fork out twenty quid?

He laid the brush aside and, laughing with delight, cried:

—Will he come? The jejune jesuit.

Ceasing, he began to shave with care.

—Tell me, Mulligan, Stephen said quietly.

—Yes, my love?

—How long is Haines going to stay in this tower?

Buck Mulligan showed a shaven cheek over his right shoulder.

—God, isn't he dreadful? he said frankly. A ponderous Saxon. He thinks you're not a gentleman. God, these bloody English.

Bursting with money and indigestion. Because he comes from Oxford. You know, Dedalus, you have the real Oxford manner. He can't make you out. O, my name for you is the best: Kinch, the knife-blade.

He shaved warily over his chin.

—He was raving all night about a black panther, Stephen said. Where is his guncase?

—A woful lunatic, Mulligan said. Were you in a funk?

—I was, Stephen said with energy and growing fear. Out here in the dark with a man I don't know raving and moaning to himself about shooting a black panther. You saved men from drowning. I'm not a hero, however. If he stays on here I am off.

Buck Mulligan frowned at the lather on his razorblade. He hopped down from his perch and began to search his trouser pockets hastily.

—Scutter, he cried thickly.

He came over to the gunrest and,

thrusting a hand into Stephen's upper pocket, said:

—Lend us a loan of your noserag to wipe my razor.

Stephen suffered him to pull out and hold up on show by its corner a dirty crumpled handkerchief. Buck Mulligan wiped the razorblade neatly. Then, gazing over the handkerchief, he said:

—The bard's noserag. A new art colour for our Irish poets: snotgreen. You can almost taste it, can't you?

He mounted to the parapet again and gazed out over Dublin bay, his fair oakpale hair stirring slightly.

—God, he said quietly. Isn't the sea what Algy calls it: a grey sweet mother? The snotgreen sea. The scrotumtightening sea. *Epi oinopa ponton.* Ah, Dedalus, the Greeks. I must teach you. You must read them in the original. *Thalatta! Thalatta!* She is our great sweet mother. Come and look.

Stephen stood up and went over to the parapet. Leaning on it he looked down on the water and on the mailboat clearing the harbour mouth of Kingstown.

—Our mighty mother, Buck Mulligan said.

He turned abruptly his great searching eyes from the sea to Stephen's face.

—The aunt thinks you killed your mother, he said. That's why she won't let me have anything to do with you.

—Someone killed her, Stephen said gloomily.

—You could have knelt down, damn it, Kinch, when your dying mother asked you, Buck Mulligan said. I'm hyperborean as much as you. But to think of your mother begging you with her last breath to kneel down and pray for her. And you refused. There is something sinister in you . . .

He broke off and lathered again lightly his farther cheek. A tolerant smile curled his lips.

—But a lovely mummer, he murmured to himself. Kinch, the loveliest mummer of them all.

He shaved evenly and with care, in silence, seriously.

Stephen, an elbow rested on the jagged granite, leaned his palm against his brow and gazed at the fraying edge of his shiny black coat-sleeve. Pain, that was not yet the pain of love, fretted his heart. Silently, in a dream she had come to him after her death, her wasted body within its loose brown graveclothes giving off an odour of wax and rosewood, her breath, that had bent upon him, mute, reproachful, a faint odour of wetted ashes. Across the threadbare cuffedge he saw the sea hailed as a great sweet mother by the wellfed voice beside him. The ring of bay and skyline held a dull green mass of liquid. A bowl of white china had stood beside her deathbed holding the green sluggish bile which she had torn up from her rotting liver by fits of loud groaning vomiting.

Buck Mulligan wiped again his razorblade.

—Ah, poor dogsbody, he said in a kind voice. I must give you a shirt and a few noserags. How are the secondhand breeks?

—They fit well enough, Stephen answered.

Buck Mulligan attacked the hollow beneath his underlip.

—The mockery of it, he said contentedly, secondleg they should be. God knows what poxy bowsy left them off. I have a lovely pair with a hair stripe, grey. You'll look spiffing in them. I'm not joking, Kinch. You look damn well when you're dressed.

—Thanks, Stephen said. I can't wear them if they are grey.

—He can't wear them, Buck Mulligan told his face in the mirror. Etiquette is etiquette.

He kills his mother but he can't wear grey trousers.

He folded his razor neatly and with stroking palps of fingers felt the smooth skin.

Stephen turned his gaze from the sea and to the plump face with its smokeblue mobile eyes.

—That fellow I was with in the Ship last night, said Buck Mulligan, says you have g.p.i. He's up in Dottyville with Conolly Norman. General paralysis of the insane.

He swept the mirror a half circle in the air to flash the tidings abroad in sunlight now radiant on the sea. His curling shaven lips laughed and the edges of his white glittering teeth. Laughter seized all his strong wellknit trunk.

—Look at yourself, he said, you dreadful bard.

Stephen bent forward and peered at the mirror held out to him, cleft by a crooked crack, hair on end. As he and others see me.

Who chose this face for me? This dogsbody
to rid of vermin. It asks me too.

—I pinched it out of the skivvy's room,
Buck Mulligan said. It does her all right. The
aunt always keeps plain-looking servants
for Malachi. Lead him not into temptation.
And her name is Ursula.

Laughing again, he brought the mirror
away from Stephen's peering eyes.

—The rage of Caliban at not seeing his
face in a mirror, he said. If Wilde were only
alive to see you.

Drawing back and pointing, Stephen said
with bitterness:

—It is a symbol of Irish art. The cracked
lookingglass of a servant.

Buck Mulligan suddenly linked his arm
in Stephen's and walked with him round
the tower, his razor and mirror clacking in
the pocket where he had thrust them.

—It's not fair to tease you like that, Kinch,
is it? he said kindly. God knows you have

more spirit than any of them.

Parried again. He fears the lancet of my art as I fear that of his. The cold steelpen.

—Cracked lookingglass of a servant. Tell that to the oxy chap downstairs and touch him for a guinea. He's stinking with money and thinks you're not a gentleman. His old fellow made his tin by selling jalap to Zulus or some bloody swindle or other. God, Kinch, if you and I could only work together we might do something for the island. Hellenise it.

Cranly's arm. His arm.

—And to think of your having to beg from these swine. I'm the only one that knows what you are. Why don't you trust me more? What have you up your nose against me? Is it Haines? If he makes any noise here I'll bring down Seymour and we'll give him a ragging worse than they gave Clive Kempthorpe.

Young shouts of moneyed voices in Clive

Kempthorpe's rooms. Palefaces: they hold their ribs with laughter, one clasping another, O, I shall expire! Break the news to her gently, Aubrey! I shall die! With slit ribbons of his shirt whipping the air he hops and hobbles round the table, with trousers down at heels, chased by Ades of Magdalen with the tailor's shears. A scared calf's face gilded with marmalade. I don't want to be debagged! Don't you play the giddy ox with me!

Shouts from the open window startling evening in the quadrangle. A deaf gardener, aproned, masked with Matthew Arnold's face, pushes his mower on the sombre lawn watching narrowly the dancing motes of grasshalms.

To ourselves . . . new paganism . . . omphalos.

—Let him stay, Stephen said. There's nothing wrong with him except at night.

—Then what is it? Buck Mulligan asked

impatiently. Cough it up. I'm quite frank with you. What have you against me now?

They halted, looking towards the blunt cape of Bray Head that lay on the water like the snout of a sleeping whale. Stephen freed his arm quietly.

—Do you wish me to tell you? he asked.

—Yes, what is it? Buck Mulligan answered. I don't remember anything.

He looked in Stephen's face as he spoke. A light wind passed his brow, fanning softly his fair uncombed hair and stirring silver points of anxiety in his eyes.

Stephen, depressed by his own voice, said:

—Do you remember the first day I went to your house after my mother's death?

Buck Mulligan frowned quickly and said:

—What? Where? I can't remember anything. I remember only ideas and sensations. Why? What happened in the name of God?

—You were making tea, Stephen said, and

I went across the landing to get more hot water. Your mother and some visitor came out of the drawingroom. She asked you who was in your room.

—Yes? Buck Mulligan said. What did I say? I forget.

—You said, Stephen answered, *O, it's only Dedalus whose mother is beastly dead.*

A flush which made him seem younger and more engaging rose to Buck Mulligan's cheek.

—Did I say that? he asked. Well? What harm is that?

He shook his constraint from him nervously.

—And what is death, he asked, your mother's or yours or my own? You saw only your mother die. I see them pop off every day in the Mater and Richmond and cut up into tripes in the dissecting room. It's a beastly thing and nothing else. It simply doesn't matter. You wouldn't kneel down to pray for your mother on her deathbed when she asked you. Why? Because you have the cursed jesuit strain in you, only it's injected the wrong way. To me it's all a mockery and beastly. Her cerebral lobes are not functioning. She calls the doctor Sir Peter Teazle and picks buttercups off the quilt. Humour her till it's over. You crossed her last wish in death and yet you sulk with me because I don't whinge like some hired mute from Lalouette's. Absurd! I suppose I did say it. I didn't mean to offend the memory of your mother.

He had spoken himself into boldness. Stephen, shielding the gaping wounds which the words had left in his heart, said very coldly:

—I am not thinking of the offence to my mother.

—Of what, then? Buck Mulligan asked.

—Of the offence to me, Stephen answered.

Buck Mulligan swung round on his heel.

—O, an impossible person! he exclaimed.

He walked off quickly round the parapet. Stephen stood at his post, gazing over the calm sea towards the headland. Sea and headland now grew dim. Pulses were beating in his eyes, veiling their sight, and he felt the fever of his cheeks.

A voice within the tower called loudly:

—Are you up there, Mulligan?

—I'm coming, Buck Mulligan answered.

He turned towards Stephen and said:

—Look at the sea. What does it care about offences? Chuck Loyola, Kinch, and come on down. The Sassenach wants his morning rashers.

His head halted again for a moment at the top of the staircase, level with the roof.

—Don't mope over it all day, he said. I'm inconsequent. Give up the moody brooding.

His head vanished but the drone of his

descending voice boomed out of the stairhead:

And no more turn aside and brood
Upon love's bitter mystery
For Fergus rules the brazen cars.

Woodshadows floated silently by
through the morning peace from the stairhead seaward where he gazed. Inshore and
farther out the mirror of water whitened,
spurned by lightshod hurrying feet. White
breast of the dim sea. The twining stresses,
two by two. A hand plucking the harp-
strings merging their twining chords.
Wavewhite wedded words shimmering on
the dim tide.

A cloud began to cover the sun slowly,
shadowing the bay in deeper green. It lay
behind him, a bowl of bitter waters. Fergus'
song: I sang it alone in the house, holding
down the long dark chords. Her door was

open: she wanted to hear my music. Silent with awe and pity I went to her bedside. She was crying in her wretched bed. For those words, Stephen: love's bitter mystery.

Where now?

Her secrets: old feather fans, tasselled dancecards, powdered with musk, a gaud of amber beads in her locked drawer. A birdcage hung in the sunny window of her house when she was a girl. She heard old Royce sing in the pantomime of Turko the terrible and laughed with others when he sang:

> *I am the boy*
> *That can enjoy*
> *Invisibility.*

Phantasmal mirth, folded away: musk perfumed.

And no more turn aside and brood

Folded away in the memory of nature with her toys. Memories beset his brooding brain. Her glass of water from the kitchen tap when she had approached the sacrament. A cored apple, filled with brown sugar, roasting for her at the hob on a dark autumn evening. Her shapely fingernails reddened by the blood of squashed lice from the children's shirts.

In a dream, silently, she had come to him, her wasted body within its loose graveclothes giving off an odour of wax and rosewood, her breath bent over him with mute secret words, a faint odour of wetted ashes.

Her glazing eyes, staring out of death, to shake and bend my soul. On me alone. The ghostcandle to light her agony. Ghostly light on the tortured face. Her hoarse loud breath rattling in horror, while all prayed on their knees. Her eyes on me to strike me down. *Liliata rutilantium te confessorum turma circumdet: iubilantium te virginum chorus excipiat.*

Ghoul! Chewer of corpses!

No mother. Let me be and let me live.

—Kinch ahoy!

Buck Mulligan's voice sang from within the tower. It came nearer up the staircase, calling again. Stephen, still trembling at his soul's cry, heard warm running sunlight and in the air behind him friendly words.

—Dedalus, come down, like a good mosey. Breakfast is ready. Haines is apologizing for waking us last night. It's all right.

—I'm coming, Stephen said, turning.

—Do, for Jesus' sake, Buck Mulligan said. For my sake and for all our sakes.

His head disappeared and reappeared.

—I told him your symbol of Irish art. He says it's very clever. Touch him for a quid, will you? A guinea, I mean.

—I get paid this morning, Stephen said.

—The school kip? Buck Mulligan said.

How much? Four quid? Lend us one.

—If you want it, Stephen said.

—Four shining sovereigns, Buck Mulligan cried with delight. We'll have a glorious drunk to astonish the druidy druids. Four omnipotent sovereigns.

He flung up his hands and tramped down the stone stairs, singing out of tune with a Cockney accent:

> *O, won't we have a merry time*
> *Drinking whisky, beer and wine,*
> *On coronation,*
> *Coronation day?*
> *O, won't we have a merry time*
> *On coronation day?*

Warm sunshine merrying over the sea. The nickel shaving-bowl shone, forgotten, on the parapet. Why should I bring it down? Or leave it there all day, forgotten friendship?

He went over to it, held it in his hands awhile, feeling its coolness, smelling the clammy slaver of the lather in which the brush was stuck. So I carried the boat of incense then at Clongowes. I am another now and yet the same. A servant too. A server of a servant.

In the gloomy domed livingroom of the tower Buck Mulligan's gowned form moved briskly about the hearth to and fro, hiding and revealing its yellow glow. Two shafts of soft daylight fell across the flagged floor from the high barbicans: and at the meeting of their rays a cloud of coalsmoke and fumes of fried grease floated, turning.

—We'll be choked, Buck Mulligan said. Haines, open that door, will you?

Stephen laid the shavingbowl on the locker. A tall figure rose from the hammock where it had been sitting, went to the doorway and pulled open the inner doors.

—Have you the key? a voice asked.

—Dedalus has it, Buck Mulligan said. Janey Mack, I'm choked. He howled without looking up from the fire:

—Kinch!

—It's in the lock, Stephen said, coming forward.

The key scraped round harshly twice and, when the heavy door had been set ajar, welcome light and bright air entered. Haines stood at the doorway, looking out. Stephen haled his upended valise to the table and sat down to wait. Buck Mulligan tossed the fry on to the dish beside him. Then he carried the dish and a large teapot over to the table, set them down heavily and sighed with relief.

—I'm melting, he said, as the candle remarked when . . . But hush. Not a word more on that subject. Kinch, wake up. Bread, butter, honey. Haines, come in. The grub is ready. Bless us, O Lord, and these thy gifts. Where's the sugar? O, jay, there's no milk.

Stephen fetched the loaf and the pot of honey and the buttercooler from the locker. Buck Mulligan sat down in a sudden pet.

—What sort of a kip is this? he said. I told her to come after eight.

—We can drink it black, Stephen said. There's a lemon in the locker.

—O, damn you and your Paris fads, Buck Mulligan said. I want Sandycove milk.

Haines came in from the doorway and said quietly:

—That woman is coming up with the milk.

—The blessings of God on you, Buck Mulligan cried, jumping up from his chair. Sit down. Pour out the tea there. The sugar is in the bag. Here, I can't go fumbling at the damned eggs. He hacked through the fry on the dish and slapped it out on three plates, saying:

—*In nomine Patris et Filii et Spiritus Sancti.*

Haines sat down to pour out the tea.

—I'm giving you two lumps each, he said. But, I say, Mulligan, you do make strong tea, don't you?

Buck Mulligan, hewing thick slices from the loaf, said in an old woman's wheedling voice:

—When I makes tea I makes tea, as old mother Grogan said. And when I makes water I makes water.

—By Jove, it is tea, Haines said.

Buck Mulligan went on hewing and wheedling:

—*So I do, Mrs Cahill*, says she. *Begob, ma'am*, says Mrs Cahill, *God send you don't make them in the one pot.*

He lunged towards his messmates in turn a thick slice of bread, impaled on his knife.

—That's folk, he said very earnestly, for your book, Haines. Five lines of text and ten pages of notes about the folk and the fish-gods of Dundrum. Printed by the weird sisters in the year of the big wind.

He turned to Stephen and asked in a fine puzzled voice, lifting his brows:

—Can you recall, brother, is mother Grogan's tea and water pot spoken of in the Mabinogion or is it in the Upanishads?

—I doubt it, said Stephen gravely.

—Do you now? Buck Mulligan said in the same tone. Your reasons, pray?

—I fancy, Stephen said as he ate, it did not exist in or out of the Mabinogion. Mother Grogan was, one imagines, a kinswoman of Mary Ann.

Buck Mulligan's face smiled with delight.

—Charming, he said in a finical sweet voice, showing his white teeth and blinking his eyes pleasantly. Do you think she was? Quite charming.

Then, suddenly overclouding all his features, he growled in a hoarsened rasping voice as he hewed again vigorously at the loaf:

—*For old Mary Ann*
She doesn't care a damn,
But, hising up her petticoats . . .

He crammed his mouth with fry and munched and droned.

The doorway was darkened by an entering form.

—The milk, sir.

—Come in, ma'am, Mulligan said. Kinch, get the jug.

An old woman came forward and stood by Stephen's elbow.

—That's a lovely morning, sir, she said. Glory be to God.

—To whom? Mulligan said, glancing at her. Ah, to be sure.

Stephen reached back and took the milkjug from the locker.

—The islanders, Mulligan said to Haines casually, speak frequently of the collector of prepuces.

34

—How much, sir? asked the old woman.

—A quart, Stephen said.

He watched her pour into the measure and thence into the jug rich white milk, not hers. Old shrunken paps. She poured again a measureful and a tilly. Old and secret she had entered from a morning world, maybe a messenger. She praised the goodness of the milk, pouring it out. Crouching by a patient cow at daybreak in the lush field, a witch on her toadstool, her wrinkled fingers quick at the squirting dugs. They lowed about her whom they knew, dewsilky cattle. Silk of the kine and poor old woman, names given her in old times. A wandering crone, lowly form of an immortal serving her conqueror and her gay betrayer, their common cuckquean, a messenger from the secret morning. To serve or to upbraid, whether he could not tell: but scorned to beg her favour.

—It is indeed, ma'am, Buck Mulligan said, pouring milk into their cups.

—Taste it, sir, she said.

He drank at her bidding.

—If we could only live on good food like that, he said to her somewhat loudly, we wouldn't have the country full of rotten teeth and rotten guts. Living in a bogswamp, eating cheap food and the streets paved with dust, horsedung and consumptives' spits.

—Are you a medical student, sir? the old woman asked.

—I am, ma'am, Buck Mulligan answered.

Stephen listened in scornful silence. She bows her old head to a voice that speaks to her loudly, her bonesetter, her medicine-man; me she slights. To the voice that will shrive and oil for the grave all there is of her but her woman's unclean loins, of man's flesh made not in God's likeness, the serpent's prey. And to the loud voice that now bids her be silent with wondering unsteady eyes.

—Do you understand what he says? Stephen asked her.

—Is it French you are talking, sir? the old woman said to Haines.

Haines spoke to her again a longer speech, confidently.

—Irish, Buck Mulligan said. Is there Gaelic on you?

—I thought it was Irish, she said, by the sound of it. Are you from west, sir?

—I am an Englishman, Haines answered.

—He's English, Buck Mulligan said, and he thinks we ought to speak Irish in Ireland.

—Sure we ought to, the old woman said, and I'm ashamed I don't speak the language myself. I'm told it's a grand language by them that knows.

—Grand is no name for it, said Buck Mulligan. Wonderful entirely. Fill us out some more tea, Kinch. Would you like a cup, ma'am?

—No, thank you, sir, the old woman said,

slipping the ring of the milkcan on her forearm and about to go.

Haines said to her:

—Have you your bill? We had better pay her, Mulligan, hadn't we?

Stephen filled the three cups.

—Bill, sir? she said, halting. Well, it's seven mornings a pint at twopence is seven twos is a shilling and twopence over and these three mornings a quart at fourpence is three quarts is a shilling and one and two is two and two, sir.

Buck Mulligan sighed and having filled his mouth with a crust thickly buttered on both sides, stretched forth his legs and began to search his trouser pockets.

—Pay up and look pleasant, Haines said to him smiling.

Stephen filled a third cup, a spoonful of tea colouring faintly the thick rich milk. Buck Mulligan brought up a florin, twisted it round in his fingers and cried:

—A miracle!

He passed it along the table towards the old woman, saying:

—Ask nothing more of me, sweet. All I can give you I give.

Stephen laid the coin in her uneager hand.

—We'll owe twopence, he said.

—Time enough, sir, she said, taking the coin. Time enough. Good morning, sir.

She curtseyed and went out, followed by Buck Mulligan's tender chant:

—*Heart of my heart, were it more,*
More would be laid at your feet.

He turned to Stephen and said:

—Seriously, Dedalus. I'm stony. Hurry out to your school kip and bring us back some money. Today the bards must drink and junket. Ireland expects that every man this day will do his duty.

—That reminds me, Haines said, rising, that I have to visit your national library today.

—Our swim first, Buck Mulligan said.

He turned to Stephen and asked blandly:

—Is this the day for your monthly wash, Kinch?

Then he said to Haines:

—The unclean bard makes a point of washing once a month.

—All Ireland is washed by the gulfstream, Stephen said as he let honey trickle over a slice of the loaf.

Haines from the corner where he was knotting easily a scarf about the loose collar of his tennis shirt spoke:

—I intend to make a collection of your sayings if you will let me.

Speaking to me. They wash and tub and scrub. Agenbite of inwit. Conscience. Yet here's a spot.

—That one about the cracked lookingglass of a servant being the symbol of Irish art is deuced good.

Buck Mulligan kicked Stephen's foot under the table and said with warmth of tone:

—Wait till you hear him on Hamlet, Haines.

—Well, I mean it, Haines said, still speaking to Stephen. I was just thinking of it when that poor old creature came in.

—Would I make money by it? Stephen asked.

Haines laughed and, as he took his soft grey hat from the holdfast of the hammock, said:

—I don't know, I'm sure.

He strolled out to the doorway. Buck Mulligan bent across to Stephen and said with coarse vigour:

—You put your hoof in it now. What did you say that for?

—Well? Stephen said. The problem is to

get money. From whom? From the milk-woman, or from him. It's a toss up, I think.

—I blow him out about you, Buck Mulligan said, and then you come along with your lousy leer and your gloomy jesuit jibes.

—I see little hope, Stephen said, from her or from him.

Buck Mulligan sighed tragically and laid his hand on Stephen's arm.

—From me, Kinch, he said.

In a suddenly changed tone he added:

—To tell you the God's truth I think you're right. Damn all else they are good for. Why don't you play them as I do? To hell with them all. Let us get out of the kip.

He stood up, gravely ungirdled and disrobed himself of his gown, saying resignedly:

—Mulligan is stripped of his garments.

He emptied his pockets on to the table.

—There's your snotrag, he said.

And putting on his stiff collar and rebellious tie, he spoke to them, chiding them, and to his dangling watchchain. His hands plunged and rummaged in his trunk while he called for a clean handkerchief. Agenbite of inwit. God, we'll simply have to dress the character. I want puce gloves and green boots. Contradiction. Do I contradict myself? Very well then, I contradict myself. Mercurial Malachi. A limp black missile flew out of his talking hands.

—And there's your Latin quarter hat, he said.

Stephen picked it up and put it on. Haines called to them from the doorway:

—Are you coming, you fellows?

—I'm ready, Buck Mulligan answered, going towards the door. Come out, Kinch. You have eaten all we left, I suppose. Resigned he passed out with grave words and gait, saying, wellnigh with sorrow:

—And going forth he met Butterly.

Stephen, taking his ashplant from its leaningplace, followed them out and, as they went down the ladder, pulled to the slow iron door and locked it. He put the huge key in his inner pocket.

At the foot of the ladder Buck Mulligan asked:

—Did you bring the key?

—I have it, Stephen said, preceding them.

He walked on. Behind him he heard Buck Mulligan club with his heavy bathtowel the leader shoots of ferns or grasses.

—Down, sir. How dare you, sir?

Haines asked:

—Do you pay rent for this tower?

—Twelve quid, Buck Mulligan said.

—To the secretary of state for war, Stephen added over his shoulder.

They halted while Haines surveyed the tower and said at last:

—Rather bleak in wintertime, I should say. Martello you call it?

—Billy Pitt had them built, Buck Mulligan said, when the French were on the sea. But ours is the *omphalos*.

—What is your idea of Hamlet? Haines asked Stephen.

—No, no, Buck Mulligan shouted in pain. I'm not equal to Thomas Aquinas and the fiftyfive reasons he has made to prop it up. Wait till I have a few pints in me first.

He turned to Stephen, saying as he pulled down neatly the peaks of his primrose waistcoat:

—You couldn't manage it under three pints, Kinch, could you?

—It has waited so long, Stephen said listlessly, it can wait longer.

—You pique my curiosity, Haines said amiably. Is it some paradox?

—Pooh! Buck Mulligan said. We have grown out of Wilde and paradoxes. It's quite simple. He proves by algebra that Hamlet's grandson is Shakespeare's grandfather and that he himself is the ghost of his own father.

—What? Haines said, beginning to point at Stephen. He himself?

Buck Mulligan slung his towel stolewise round his neck and, bending in loose laughter, said to Stephen's ear:

—O, shade of Kinch the elder! Japhet in search of a father!

—We're always tired in the morning, Stephen said to Haines. And it is rather long to tell.

Buck Mulligan, walking forward again, raised his hands.

—The sacred pint alone can unbind the tongue of Dedalus, he said.

—I mean to say, Haines explained to Stephen as they followed, this tower and these cliffs here remind me somehow of Elsinore. *That beetles o'er his base into the sea*, isn't it?

Buck Mulligan turned suddenly for an

instant towards Stephen but did not speak.
In the bright silent instant Stephen saw his
own image in cheap dusty mourning
between their gay attires.

—It's a wonderful tale, Haines said,
bringing them to halt again.

Eyes, pale as the sea the wind had fresh-
ened, paler, firm and prudent. The seas'
ruler, he gazed southward over the bay,
empty save for the smokeplume of the mailboat, vague on the bright skyline, and a sail
tacking by the Muglins.

—I read a theological interpretation of it
somewhere, he said bemused. The Father
and the Son idea. The Son striving to be
atoned with the Father.

Buck Mulligan at once put on a blithe
broadly smiling face. He looked at them, his
wellshaped mouth open happily, his eyes,
from which he had suddenly withdrawn all
shrewd sense, blinking with mad gaiety. He
moved a doll's head to and fro, the brims

of his Panama hat quivering, and began to chant in a quiet happy foolish voice:

—*I'm the queerest young fellow that ever*
  you heard.
My mother's a jew, my father's a bird.
With Joseph the joiner I cannot agree,
So here's to disciples and Calvary.

He held up a forefinger of warning.

—*If anyone thinks that I amn't divine*
He'll get no free drinks when I'm making
  the wine
But have to drink water and wish it were
  plain
That I make when the wine becomes water
  again.

He tugged swiftly at Stephen's ashplant in farewell and, running forward to a brow of the cliff, fluttered his hands at his sides

like fins or wings of one about to rise in the
air, and chanted:

—*Goodbye, now, goodbye. Write down all
I said
And tell Tom, Dick and Harry I rose from
the dead.
What's bred in the bone cannot fail me to
fly
And Olivet's breezy ... Goodbye, now,
goodbye.*

He capered before them down towards
the fortyfoot hole, fluttering his winglike
hands, leaping nimbly, Mercury's hat quivering in the fresh wind that bore back to
them his brief birdlike cries.

Haines, who had been laughing guard-
edly, walked on beside Stephen and said:

—We oughtn't to laugh, I suppose. He's
rather blasphemous. I'm not a believer
myself, that is to say. Still his gaiety takes

the harm out of it somehow, doesn't it? What did he call it? Joseph the Joiner?

—The ballad of Joking Jesus, Stephen answered.

—O, Haines said, you have heard it before?

—Three times a day, after meals, Stephen said drily.

—You're not a believer, are you? Haines asked. I mean, a believer in the narrow sense of the word. Creation from nothing and miracles and a personal God.

—There's only one sense of the word, it seems to me, Stephen said.

Haines stopped to take out a smooth silver case in which twinkled a green stone. He sprang it open with his thumb and offered it.

—Thank you, Stephen said, taking a cigarette.

Haines helped himself and snapped the case to. He put it back in his sidepocket and took from his waistcoatpocket a nickel tinderbox, sprang it open too, and, having lit his cigarette, held the flaming spunk towards Stephen in the shell of his hands.

—Yes, of course, he said, as they went on again. Either you believe or you don't, isn't it? Personally I couldn't stomach that idea of a personal God. You don't stand for that, I suppose?

—You behold in me, Stephen said with grim displeasure, a horrible example of free thought.

He walked on, waiting to be spoken to, trailing his ashplant by his side. Its ferrule followed lightly on the path, squealing at his heels. My familiar, after me, calling Steeeeeeeeeephen. A wavering line along the path. They will walk on it tonight, coming here in the dark. He wants that key. It is mine, I paid the rent. Now I eat his salt bread. Give him the key too. All. He will ask for it. That was in his eyes.

—After all, Haines began . . .

Stephen turned and saw that the cold gaze which had measured him was not all unkind.

—After all, I should think you are able to free yourself. You are your own master, it seems to me.

—I am the servant of two masters, Stephen said, an English and an Italian.

—Italian? Haines said.

A crazy queen, old and jealous. Kneel down before me.

—And a third, Stephen said, there is who wants me for odd jobs.

—Italian? Haines said again. What do you mean?

—The imperial British state, Stephen answered, his colour rising, and the holy Roman catholic and apostolic church.

Haines detached from his underlip some fibres of tobacco before he spoke.

—I can quite understand that, he said

calmly. An Irishman must think like that, I daresay. We feel in England that we have treated you rather unfairly. It seems history is to blame.

The proud potent titles clanged over Stephen's memory the triumph of their brazen bells: *et unam sanctam catholicam et apostolicam ecclesiam*: the slow growth and change of rite and dogma like his own rare thoughts, a chemistry of stars. Symbol of the apostles in the mass for pope Marcellus, the voices blended, singing alone loud in affirmation: and behind their chant the vigilant angel of the church militant disarmed and menaced her heresiarchs. A horde of heresies fleeing with mitres awry: Photius and the brood of mockers of whom Mulligan was one, and Arius, warring his life long upon the consubstantiality of the Son with the Father, and Valentine, spurning Christ's terrene body, and the subtle African heresiarch Sabellius who held that the Father was Himself His own Son. Words Mulligan had spoken a moment since in mockery to the stranger. Idle mockery. The void awaits surely all them that weave the wind: a menace, a disarming and a worsting from those embattled angels of the church, Michael's host, who defend her ever in the hour of conflict with their lances and their shields.

Hear, hear. Prolonged applause. *Zut ! Nom de Dieu!*

—Of course I'm a Britisher, Haines' voice said, and I feel as one. I don't want to see my country fall into the hands of German jews either. That's our national problem, I'm afraid, just now.

Two men stood at the verge of the cliff, watching: businessman, boatman.

—She's making for Bullock harbour.

The boatman nodded towards the north of the bay with some disdain.

—There's five fathoms out there, he said.

It'll be swept up that way when the tide comes in about one. It's nine days today.

The man that was drowned. A sail veering about the blank bay waiting for a swollen bundle to bob up, roll over to the sun a puffy face, salt white. Here I am.

They followed the winding path down to the creek. Buck Mulligan stood on a stone, in shirtsleeves, his unclipped tie rippling over his shoulder. A young man clinging to a spur of rock near him moved slowly frogwise his green legs in the deep jelly of the water.

—Is the brother with you, Malachi?

—Down in Westmeath. With the Bannons.

—Still there? I got a card from Bannon. Says he found a sweet young thing down there. Photo girl he calls her

—Snapshot, eh? Brief exposure.

Buck Mulligan sat down to unlace his boots. An elderly man shot up near the spur

of rock a blowing red face. He scrambled up
by the stones, water glistening on his pate
and on its garland of grey hair, water rilling
over his chest and paunch and spilling jets
out of his black sagging loincloth.

Buck Mulligan made way for him to
scramble past and, glancing at Haines and
Stephen, crossed himself piously with his
thumbnail at brow and lips and breast-
bone.

—Seymour's back in town, the young
man said, grasping again his spur of rock.
Chucked medicine and going in for the
army.

—Ah, go to God, Buck Mulligan said.

—Going over next week to stew. You
know that red Carlisle girl, Lily?

—Yes.

—Spooning with him last night on the
pier. The father is rotto with money.

—Is she up the pole?

—Better ask Seymour that.

—Seymour a bleeding officer, Buck Mulligan said.

He nodded to himself as he drew off his trousers and stood up, saying tritely:

—Redheaded women buck like goats.

He broke off in alarm, feeling his side under his flapping shirt.

—My twelfth rib is gone, he cried. I'm the *Uebermensch*. Toothless Kinch and I, the supermen.

He struggled out of his shirt and flung it behind him to where his clothes lay.

—Are you going in here, Malachi?

—Yes. Make room in the bed.

The young man shoved himself backward through the water and reached the middle of the creek in two long clean strokes. Haines sat down on a stone, smoking.

—Are you not coming in? Buck Mulligan asked.

—Later on, Haines said. Not on my breakfast.

Stephen turned away.

—I'm going, Mulligan, he said.

—Give us that key, Kinch, Buck Mulligan said, to keep my chemise flat.

Stephen handed him the key. Buck Mulligan laid it across his heaped clothes.

—And twopence, he said, for a pint. Throw it there.

Stephen threw two pennies on the soft heap. Dressing, undressing. Buck Mulligan erect, with joined hands before him, said solemnly:

—He who stealeth from the poor lendeth to the Lord. Thus spake Zarathustra.

His plump body plunged.

—We'll see you again, Haines said, turning as Stephen walked up the path and smiling at wild Irish.

Horn of a bull, hoof of a horse, smile of a Saxon.

—The Ship, Buck Mulligan cried. Half twelve.

—Good, Stephen said.

He walked along the upwardcurving path.

Liliata rutilantium.
Turma circumdet.
Iubilantium te virginum

The priest's grey nimbus in a niche where he dressed discreetly. I will not sleep here tonight. Home also I cannot go.

A voice, sweettoned and sustained, called to him from the sea. Turning the curve he waved his hand. It called again. A sleek brown head, a seal's, far out on the water, round.

Usurper.

WHS LITTLE READS

£1 voucher

**£1.00 OFF WHEN YOU BUY THE
FULL-LENGTH EDITION OF THIS BOOK✱**

To the Customer: Present this voucher at participating
WHSmith stores and redeem it for £1.00 off the price of
the full-length edition of Ulysses✱.

Terms & Conditions: 1. This voucher entitles you to
£1.00 off the price of the full-length edition of
Ulysses✱. 2. Offer valid in participating WHSmith High
Street and Travel stores, subject to availability, while
stocks last. 3. Voucher valid from
19 April 2003 until 31 March 2004 inclusive.
4. Cannot be exchanged for any other merchandise.
5. Only one voucher per transaction. 6. Only original,
unaltered vouchers will be accepted. WHSmith reserves
the right to reject any voucher it deems, in its sole
discretion, to have been forged, defaced or otherwise
tampered with. 7. Cash redemption value 0.001p.
Promoter: WH Smith Retail Limited, Greenbridge Road,
Swindon, Wiltshire SN3 3RX.
✱ Subject to a minimum R.R.P. of £2.50

**TO THE STORE: PLEASE SCAN VOUCHER AND PRODUCT.
DO NOT 'MINT RETURN'. DESTROY VOUCHER.**